SCOOBY-DOO! and YOU:

THE CASE OF THE MONSTROUS MUTT

A Collect the Clues Mystery

By Jenny Markas

WORLDWIDE PUBLISHING™

SCHOLASTIC INC.

New York   Toronto   London   Auckland   Sydney
Mexico City   New Delhi   Hong Kong

ISBN 0-439-23158-2

12 11 10 9 8 7 6 5 4 3   2 3 4 5 6/0

Cover and interior illustrations by Duendes del Sur
Cover and interior design by Madalina Stefan

Printed in the U.S.A.

First Scholastic printing, March 2001

"Wow, that looks great!" Fred is staring at a big pile of fruit that Serena is tossing into the blender. "Bananas, mango, pineapple, and — what's that orange stuff?"

"Papaya," says Serena with a big smile. "It's good for you." Serena has bright purple hair and big blue eyes and the dress she's wearing has patterns in every color of the rainbow.

You've joined Scooby and the gang here to check out the smoothies. An article in the

1

local newspaper said they were the best frozen fruit drinks anywhere.

"Like, awesome," Shaggy says. "But, like, can we get other stuff besides fruit in those drinks?"

"Sure," Serena says. "What did you have in mind?"

"Rookies!" Scooby says, from beside Shaggy.

Serena looks bewildered.

"Cookies," Velma explains.

Serena giggles. "Well, I never heard of a chocolate-chip cookie smoothie, but if you'll drink it, I'll make it. Wait right here." She takes off her apron and runs into the store next door. A minute later, she comes out with a bag of chocolate-chip cookies.

"Here goes," she says, putting her apron back on and starting up the blender. "We'll add some bananas, some nice cold milk, and —" She pours the shake into two paper cups and hands one each to Scooby and Shaggy. "What do you think?" she asks, as they each take a sip.

"Most excellent," Shaggy says.

"Rum, rum," Scooby agrees.

Serena just smiles and shakes her head. "Guess I have a new flavor to offer," she says. "Who's next?"

Daphne, Velma, and you each order a smoothie. None of you goes for the cookie flavor. That's just too wild for you!

Then you take your shakes over to the picnic table nearby and sit down to sip and enjoy. "So," you say, as you taste your banana-strawberry-apricot smoothie, "have you guys solved any mysteries lately?"

"Funny you should ask," Fred says. "We just wrapped one up. It was a doggone tough

mystery! If you'd like to read about it, you can look through our Clue Keeper."

"I took all the notes," Daphne adds. " I did a good job, too. You'll find everything you need there if you want to try to solve the mystery yourself. I marked each suspect with a , and each clue with a ."

"Not only that," Velma says. "There's a list of questions at the end of some Clue Keeper entries. You can borrow my pen if you want, and write down the answers in your own Clue Keeper."

Shaggy slurps down the last bit of his smoothie. "Like, that was *delicious!*" He jumps up. "Want another one, Scooby? All that detective work made me thirsty."

Scooby nods quickly. *"Rou-bet!"*

"What flavor should we get this time?" Shaggy asks, as the two of them head back to Serena's stand. "I'm thinking, like, chocolate bar peanut crunch. Does that sound good?"

Scooby nods again.

You look back at Fred, Velma, and Daphne, and the four of you break into laughter. Shaggy and Scooby are too much! When you finally stop laughing and catch your breath, you reach for the Clue Keeper. It's time to try to solve *The Case of the Monstrous Mutt.*

Clue Keeper Entry 1

"'I love my Doberman pinscher,'" Fred read a bumper sticker out loud.

"'Pomeranians rule!'" Velma giggled as she read another one. "That's funny. Aren't Pomeranians those teensy little dogs?"

"Teensy, but ferocious," said a woman who had just climbed out of the RV that was decorated with that bumper sticker. In her arms was a small, orange-colored ball of fluff. "Right, Pookums?" she asked, nuzzling the tiny dog's face.

"He's not ferocious at all!" I said. "He's absolutely adorable."

"Shhh!" the woman said. "He thinks he's a guard dog. Don't hurt his feelings!"

We all laughed as we strolled away, down the aisle of parked RV's and cars. These belonged to the exhibitors, the people who would be showing their purebred, pedigreed dogs at the Brownsville Dog Show. The show wasn't scheduled to start until the next day. But a man named Major Barkingham had phoned to ask us to come down ahead of time.

"There you are!" called the Major, a tall, thin man with gray hair and a big, bristly gray mustache to match. "You must be the Mystery, Inc. folks. I recognize you from your picture in the paper after your last case. I'm Major Barkingham. Welcome, welcome." He hurried toward us, smiling warmly.

"Hello, Major," I said, shaking his hand. I introduced myself and my friends.

"I'm so delighted you could come," he said loudly as he hurried us along the rows of parked cars spilling more owners and dogs. I thought his English accent was adorable and he seemed so friendly. I liked him.

He led us through a big, empty red-and-white striped tent. "This is where the obedience events will take place," he explained. Then we followed him into an even bigger yellow-and-white tent, with big squares marked off with ropes. "We'll have the conformation trials in here," he told us.

"The what?" Shaggy asked.

"*Ruh?*" Scooby looked confused, too.

"That's where people show their dogs to a judge. The judge decides which dog best represents its breed. Then the winners of each breed compete for best-in-show. Wait until you see all the beautiful dogs parading around in here tomorrow."

As he spoke, he led us through the yellow tent and into a small building behind it. He opened a door marked DIRECTOR and showed us in. "This is my office," he told us. "Please, have a seat."

I looked around and noticed that every wall in the office was covered with pictures of dogs and their owners. Big dogs, little dogs, fluffy dogs, sporty-looking dogs. "You must really love dogs," I said.

"I do," he answered a little sadly. "And I love putting on this show. Once a year, all the dog owners from every nearby state travel here to show off their dogs. I split the money I raise from the show and give half to the Humane Society. The other half goes to pay the taxes on this land, so I can let the town children use it as a recreation field. Local people like to walk their dogs here, too."

"That sounds terrific!" Velma said.

Major Barkingham sighed. "It is. Or at least, it was. This may be the last show I put on."

"Why?" Fred asked.

"Because someone doesn't want me to have the dog show here anymore," the Major answered, pulling a piece of paper out of a drawer. "See what they sent me?"

It was a poem, printed in big, dark letters.

DIRTY TRICKS, A NASTY SURPRISE,

A MONSTROUS MUTT WITH FIERY EYES!

CANCEL THE SHOW IF THESE YOU FEAR,

AND THE MONSTROUS MUTT WILL DISAPPEAR!

The note was signed with a gigantic pawprint, even bigger than Scooby's paw.

"Wow," I said. "Who could have sent that?"

"That's why I phoned you," the Major said. "I hear you're good detectives. Maybe you can help me."

10

"Like, we'll definitely try," Shaggy said.

Scooby nodded in agreement.

Just then, there was a knock at the door. A small, dark-haired woman in overalls stepped in. "Where are the electrical cords you promised me?" she asked. "I can't find anything around here, with all these dogs arriving."

"Come in, Josie," the Major said to her. He introduced each of us to the woman, whose name was Josie McBee. "Josie runs the community theatre in town," he said. "She's helping me out with some of the lighting and sound for the show."

"Not because I want to," Josie said to him. "Kids and animals are *not* my favorite causes. You know I think this property would be much better for a summer theater than for a dumb dog show. But you do pay well. So I'll do the job."

I glanced over at Scooby to see if she had hurt his feelings. He looked a little upset, but I heard Shaggy promise him a Scooby Snack and he brightened right up.

The Major got up to help Josie find her equipment. "I'll see you all later," he said. "Go ahead and look around, and don't forget what we talked about. I hope you can help me."

"We'll do our best," Fred promised.

Fred's Mystery-Solving Tips

"**W**ow! I can hardly wait for the dog show to begin! Did you happen to see the 👁👁 in this Clue Keeper Entry? Great. That means you can probably answer these questions."

1. What is the suspect's name?

2. What does the suspect do for a living?

3. Why would the suspect want the Major's dog show shut down?

"Did you get all the answers? Excellent. Then let's go meet some of the dogs that are here for the show."

Clue Keeper Entry 2

When we arrived at the dog show site the next morning, we couldn't believe our eyes. It wasn't easy to find a place to park the Mystery Machine. Instead of just a few RV's and cars unloading dogs, there were hundreds! Everywhere we looked there were dogs of every size and color and description. I never saw so many dogs in my life.

A whole tent city had sprung up on the show grounds. There were food vendors as well as people who sold all types of dog accessories and souvenirs. I saw Scooby and

Shaggy sniffing in the direction of the food court. The smell of french fries was in the air.

"Like, let's go check out what kind of goodies they're selling," Shaggy said to Scooby.

"You just had breakfast," I reminded them, before they could run off. "Let's look around a little, first."

"And keep your eyes open," Velma added. "Remember, we have a mystery to solve."

We made our way toward the main arena. "Boy, these pooches are pampered!" Fred said as we walked through a smaller blue-and-white striped tent next to the big red-and-white one we'd seen the day before. Every dog was being bathed, shampooed, conditioned, brushed, and combed to perfection.

Just then, Major Barkingham appeared, smiling warmly. "This is the grooming area," he explained. "This is where the owners get their dogs ready to go into the judging ring." He pointed to a small, fluffy white dog sitting on a table while its owner used a blow dryer to arrange its curls just so. "That's a West Highland white terrier," he said. "One of my favorite breeds."

"That's right, you favor the smaller breeds, just like your judges!" said a short, round woman who happened to be walking by.

The Major stared at her. "Excuse me?" he asked.

"I'm Winifred Slate, of Big Dog Kennels,"

she said. "I've come to this show for the last three years, and every year it's the same. My dogs do well in their own breed contests, but when it comes to best-in-show, your judges always go for the silly little fluff-ball dogs. If you ask me, this show is rigged." She paused to take a sip from a bottle of soda pop.

"Oh?" the Major said politely. "I'm terribly sorry that you feel that way. What kind of dogs do you have?"

"Great Danes," she said proudly. She turned and yelled to someone across the tent. "Percival, bring Griselda over here!"

Moments later a boy appeared, holding a leash. At the other end was a huge, silvery dog with a shiny coat, beautiful pointed ears, and lovely dark eyes. "This is my son Percival, and this is our champion, Griselda," said Winifred Slate.

"Row!" I heard from behind me. I turned and saw Scooby. He was gazing at Griselda with an unmistakable look in his eyes.

Could it be? Was Scooby in love?

"**J**inkies! I never knew how exciting a dog show could be. I love seeing all the different breeds. It's not easy to keep my mind on the mystery. But I bet you haven't forgotten to watch for suspects! Did you see the 👁 👁 on page 17? Great! Then try to answer the following questions."

1. What is the suspect's name?

2. Why is the suspect at the dog show?

3. Why would the suspect want to shut the dog show down?

18

Clue Keeper Entry 3

"Griselda is a beautiful dog," I said.

"Of course she is," Winifred Slate said proudly. "Her father was the world-famous Great Dane named Lancelot." She gave Griselda a little pat on the head. "Okay, take her back to our spot, Percival. No need to tire her out before she goes into the judging ring. You can bring me another bottle of soda after you get her settled."

Percival led Griselda away. I thought I heard Scooby sigh as he watched her go.

"Like, how about getting some fries now?" Shaggy asked.

Scooby didn't seem to hear him. He was still watching Griselda walk away.

"Anybody else interested?" Shaggy pleaded.

"Not now," Velma said. "I want to look around some more. I love seeing all the different dogs. Look, there's a big one with a long, fluffy tail, and it's right next to a little one that doesn't have a tail at all!"

"The one with the fluffy tail is an Alaskan malamute," explained the Major. "They're sometimes trained to pull sleds through the snow."

"Cool!" Fred said.

"And the one without a tail is a corgi. It actually has a tail, but it's very short."

"He's cute," I said.

We walked into the yellow tent where the Major pointed out his favorite breeds. Some of the dogs were in the rings being judged by then, and we stopped to watch while the Major left to check in at his office. Seven basset hounds paraded around, led by men and women dressed in their best clothes.

The dogs' long ears flopped as they trotted along.

A judge, dressed in a navy blue suit, stood watching each dog as it passed him. Then he took a closer look at each dog in turn. Finally, he had the people trot the dogs around again. Then he pointed at one of the basset hounds. "First place," he said. The people watching started to clap.

"I don't know how he can tell the difference," Fred said. "They all look great to me."

"And, like, those fries *smell* pretty great to me," Shaggy said. "Isn't it time for lunch *yet*?"

He finally convinced us. We headed over to the food court and got into line at Harvey Harmon's House of Hot Dogs and Hamburgers. The line leading to the window of a silver trailer was long, but it moved fast. "You're doing a good business," I said to the burly, black-haired man who was working at the window. His name tag read HARVEY, so I figured he must be the owner.

"I'd do better if I could build a permanent store here," he grumbled, after he took our order. "But old Barkingham refuses to sell me the land."

"Isn't there somewhere else in town where you could have a store?" Velma asked.

"Sure, but this is the best spot. All the kids play on this field, and they love my fries."

"Like, I can see why," Shaggy said. He'd just tried one of the fries the man had handed over. "These are awesome!"

"Tell it to the Major," said Harvey Harmon.

We promised we would. Then we took our food and headed back to see more of the dog show.

"Like, these fries are the grooviest. But we left the food court too fast. I wanted to try the sno-cones, too. And the fried dough. And maybe a burrito or two. Oh, well, we'll go back later. Oops! I was too busy eating to notice any new suspects. Did you see the 👁 👁? Like, if you did, maybe you can help me out by answering these questions."

1. What is the suspect's name?

2. What does the suspect do for a living?

3. Why would the suspect want to shut down the dog show?

"Like, great job! Keep it up and we'll solve this dog-gone mystery in no time!"

24

Clue Keeper Entry 4

As we walked toward the red-and-white striped tent, I heard a voice over the loudspeaker. "Dog number forty-five, dog number forty-five, you're due in ring seven."

"Where's ring seven?" Fred asked.

"Right there," Velma said, pointing toward an area beneath the tent. A large number seven was posted on a pole at one corner. A woman was rushing toward the ring, hurrying her black-and-white dog along with her. "That's a springer spaniel," Velma said. "My aunt used to have one."

"I don't see any other springer spaniels around," Fred said.

"That's because this is an obedience trial, not a conformation trial." I turned to see the Major walking up behind us. "All different breeds can enter this trial."

We joined a crowd of people who were watching as the handler took her springer spaniel into the ring. "That dog is so well behaved," I said.

The Major nodded. "Wonderful, isn't it?" He looked sad. "I'm sure going to miss hosting this show."

"Miss it?" I asked. "But everything's going smoothly so far."

But, no sooner did I finish my sentence, than we all heard a tremendous racket at the other end of the tent. There was a loud, clanking noise and a sound like a steam whistle. Dozens of dogs began to bark, and people screamed.

"Like, what's that?" Shaggy asked, looking up from his fries.

"I — I think it must be the Monstrous Mutt," said the Major. His face went pale. Sure enough — the crowd surged toward

us, chased by a gigantic, clanking, stomping smoke-breathing robot dog, with laserlike red eyes and gleaming teeth of shiny metal!

The Monstrous Mutt clanked along without stopping, its huge metal feet crashing into the ground and its metal head swinging from side to side. Its eyes flashed brightly — a glowing red.

Smoke poured from the Monstrous Mutt's mouth as it let out a horrifying growl. It pawed at the ground with its big feet, and I

saw that each foot said DOG on it, as if the robot's maker had named it.

Soon the whole tent was empty. Nobody wanted to be anywhere near the Monstrous Mutt. The robot-dog never stopped. It just kept on clanking along, growling and sending out bursts of steam, until it disappeared out of sight.

"Oh, dear, oh, dear," the Major said, shaking his head. "This is just what I was worried about. That mutt is going to shut down my show!"

"We can't let that happen," Fred said.

"We'll find out where that mutt came from, and who sent you that note," Velma promised. She turned to me. "Why don't we split up and look for clues? You and Fred can check the grooming tent. I'll find Shaggy and Scooby and investigate the big building. We can meet up in the food court and compare notes."

"Sounds like a plan!" Fred said. "Don't worry, Major. We'll put that mutt in the doghouse!"

Clue Keeper Entry 5

Fred and I hurried off while Velma ran to find Scooby and Shaggy. The grooming tent was as busy as ever when we arrived. The noise of blow-dryers made it hard to hear anything else. The smell of shampoo and conditioner filled the air.

But there was another dog smell, as well. The scent of *hot dogs*. (The kind in a bun.) Harvey Harmon was making a special delivery as we walked in.

"Look!" I said. "That poodle has curlers in

its hair!" A tiny toy poodle stood on a nearby table, wearing blue curlers. Its owner was spraying it with something that smelled a lot like perfume.

Suddenly, I heard a scream from the far end of the grooming tent. "Eeek! This is a disaster!" shouted a woman's voice.

Fred and I worked our way through the aisles to see what was going on.

"How could this happen?" screeched a large woman with curly red hair. She was gesturing at her dog, a beautiful fluffy chow chow with a coat almost the same color as her owner's hair.

"What?" I asked.

"Look!" She turned the dog around so we could see its other side. There was a big splotch of white all over its red fur. "I was using my blow-dryer to dry Angel's coat, and all of a sudden it started spewing white paint! Somebody booby-trapped my blowdryer!" She was furious, and I could understand why.

"I think this is one of those 'dirty tricks' in the note the Major got," I whispered to Fred.

"Let's go find Scooby, Shaggy, and Velma and see if they've found any clues."

As we headed back to the food court, I spotted Winifred Slate walking ahead of us with Griselda on a leash. She seemed to be hurrying toward the food court as well.

Or was she just hurrying *away* from the grooming tent?

As she passed a large trash barrel, I saw her throw something into it and heard a *clunk*.

I checked the barrel when we went by. It

was full of all kinds of trash, from paper plates, to empty soda pop bottles, to handfuls of dog hair. But, near the top, I spied something very interesting.

An empty can of white paint.

"Crazy things are happening at this dog show. We have to help the Major! Do you have any ideas? Maybe you spotted a ⟶ in the last entry. If you did, you've found a clue! Try to answer these questions in your own Clue Keeper."

1. What clue did you find in this entry?

2. Which of the suspects might have been responsible for this clue?

3. How do you know?

"If you know the answers, you might be on your way to solving this mystery!"

Clue Keeper Entry 6

Meanwhile, Velma caught up to Scooby and Shaggy at the food court. They were waiting in a long line in front of the sno-cone stand. (She told me all that happened when we met up again.)

"Like, I'm thinking blue raspberry," Shaggy said, studying the sign that listed all the flavors. "What do you think?"

"Roo raspberry," Scooby agreed, nodding.

"What are you two doing?" Velma asked, her hands on her hips. "You're supposed to be looking for clues!"

"Oops!" Scooby put his head down and looked up at Velma guiltily.

"Oops," Shaggy said. "Like we were just about to work on that. But we have to keep our energy up, don't we?"

Velma shook her head. "Honestly, Shaggy," she said. "Come on. Let's go!"

"But I can almost taste it—the sno-cone that got away!" Shaggy wailed.

Just then, Josie McBee hurried by, carrying a huge coil of wire. "Excuse me! Excuse me!" she said as she worked her way through the crowd. She didn't even glance at all the beautiful dogs in the area. As she passed Shaggy, he stepped to the right just as she stepped to the left. They bumped into each other. "Teenagers!" muttered Josie, shaking her head. "Always in the way. Good for nothing. Just like dogs. Who needs them?"

She disappeared behind Harvey Harmon's silver trailer.

"Hmm . . . I wonder where she's headed," Velma said. "Let's follow her." She and Shaggy started off. "Come on, Scooby," she

36

called over her shoulder. Scooby stayed right where he was.

"Scooby?" Velma asked. She and Shaggy went back and found Scooby gazing off in the opposite direction. He didn't even seem to hear his name. "Scooby!" Velma said again. She followed his gaze and saw — Griselda! She and Winifred Slate were waiting in line for burritos.

"Scooby," Velma said, "we have a mystery to solve!"

Reluctantly, Scooby turned to follow Velma. They joined Shaggy and walked behind Harvey Harmon's trailer to see where Josie McBee had gone. There was no sign of Josie when they got there. All they saw was a huge pile of trash. There were empty cartons from hot dog rolls, used-up jugs of ketchup and mustard, and a row of huge tin cans.

"Like, check out these cans!" Shaggy said, scratching his head. "They look familiar, but I can't figure out where I saw them before."

Velma took a closer look at the giant cans. "'Hot-dog relish,'" she read off the label. "I know what you mean, Shaggy. They do look familiar."

Scooby was still looking back toward the food court. He didn't seem interested at all in solving the mystery. He was still thinking about Griselda. Suddenly, his ears pricked up.

"What's that noise?" Velma asked, a second later.

"Sounds like a cat," Shaggy said.

"Sounds like *lots* of cats!" Velma said.

Sure enough, there was a huge racket coming from the big yellow-and-white striped tent. Cats were yowling, dogs were barking, and people were yelling.

"Let's go check it out!" Shaggy said. The three of them ran toward the big tent.

Velma's Mystery-Solving Tips

"It took a while to convince Shaggy and Scooby to help, but I think we found a clue. Did you see the 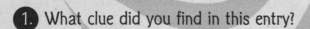? Maybe you can help figure out how this clue fits into the big picture."

1. What clue did you find in this entry?

2. Which of the suspects might have been responsible for the clue?

3. What does this clue have to do with the Monstrous Mutt?

Clue Keeper Entry 7

Fred and I ran into Shaggy, Scooby, and Velma just outside the yellow-and-white tent. We had heard the horrible noise when we were on our way to the food court to meet them.

"What *is* that?" I asked, holding my hands over my ears.

"It looks like someone has let a whole bunch of cats into the show area!" Fred said.

"Bingo!" Harvey Harmon said. He had turned up next to us. He must have run over from the food court when he heard the noise. "Isn't it hilarious?" He laughed as he watched the confusion inside the tent.

"A nasty surprise," I said, remembering the note the Major had shown us.

Harvey Harmon stared at me for a second. Then he turned back to watch the commotion.

There must have been twenty cats in that tent. Black cats, white cats, tiger-striped cats. Long-haired cats and short-haired

cats. Big fat cats and quick little kittens. And the dogs were chasing them all over, dragging their handlers along as they dashed around the tent. The cats were too quick and smart to get caught; they jumped up onto tables, climbed up tent poles, and ducked between people's legs. But meanwhile, the carefully groomed dogs were getting all messed up, and so were the carefully dressed handlers.

"This is a disaster!" cried the Major, joining us. He took Harvey Harmon's place; Harvey must have run back to the food court. "Maybe it's time to cancel this show after all."

"No!" Velma cried. "Don't do that. We're on our way to solving the mystery."

"Velma's right," I said. "Besides, it can't get any worse than this!"

I was wrong. It *did* get worse. Because that's when the Monstrous Mutt appeared again.

"Look out!" Shaggy cried, as the giant, clanking robot dog stomped into the tent.

Scooby jumped into Shaggy's arms!

Just then, an orange-and-white cat dashed past, chased by none other than Griselda. Scooby jumped out of Shaggy's arms and stood there with his chest puffed out, trying to look brave. But when the Monstrous Mutt came up behind Griselda and let out a puff of smoke and a loud growl, Scooby and Shaggy took off running. Scooby didn't even look back.

Big, beautiful Griselda turned and growled

right back at the Monstrous Mutt. Surprise!
The Mutt backed up and went off in another
direction.

The rest of us ran after Scooby and
Shaggy. "Wait!" Fred yelled. "We have to
solve the mystery!"

We screeched to a halt next to Scooby
and Shaggy, who had taken cover behind
the big silver van with Harvey Harmon's logo
on its side.

"Shaggy, it's time to stop hiding and look
for clues," I said.

"Like, I think we just found one," Shaggy said, pointing into the open door of the van. The inside of the van was covered with dark gray carpeting — and the carpeting was covered with cat hair!

Shaggy and Scooby's

Mystery-Solving Tips

"Like, everybody thinks we're afraid of that Monstrous Mutt because we ran away. But we were really just looking for clues! I think we found one, too. Did you? If you saw the 🔦 , you can probably answer these questions."

1. What clue did you find in this entry?

2. Which suspect might be responsible for this clue?

3. How does this clue fit with the other clues?

"Cool! Now, can we go get those sno-cones?"

47

Clue Keeper Entry 8

"I think it's about time we solved this case once and for all," Fred said. "I have a hunch that Monstrous Mutt isn't nearly as scary as he looks. Anybody up for helping me prove my hunch?"

"Definitely!" I said.

"I'm in!" Velma said.

Scooby and Shaggy looked doubtful. "Well . . ." Shaggy paused. "Like, exactly how are we going to prove it?"

"I have a terrific idea," Fred said.

"Like, that's what I'm afraid of," Shaggy muttered.

48

"We'll set a trap. If you dress up in your best clothes and put a number on your arm, you'll look just like one of the other handlers. And then all we have to do is get Scooby all cleaned up with some shampoo and conditioner and maybe a little blow-dry styling —"

"*Ro ray!*" Scooby said, holding up his paws and backing away.

"That's what I say," Shaggy echoed. "No way!"

"Come on, guys, it's important!" I said.

"Shaggy, you've got to help!" Velma pleaded.

"Well . . . okay. If Scooby's game." Shaggy gave in.

But Scooby stood firm, his arms folded across his chest.

"Please, Scooby?" Velma asked.

He shook his head.

"Will you do it for a Scooby Snack?" I asked. He didn't answer. He just shook his head. "How about two Scooby Snacks?" I asked.

He looked a little less firm.

"Two Scooby Snacks and one of each flavor of sno-cone," Velma promised. "How's that?"

"*Rokay!*" Scooby was smiling now. Velma tossed him two Scooby Snacks and he caught them and gulped them down. Then it was off to the grooming tent.

A little while later, Shaggy and Scooby came out, looking completely different. Shaggy wore a nice brown suit and a white shirt, and his hair was carefully combed. If not for his bright purple tie, we might not have rec-

ognized him. Beside him, Scooby was gleaming from head to toe.

"You guys look great!" I cried.

Shaggy blushed. Scooby puffed out his chest and strutted around, showing off.

"We're heading into the red-and-white obedience tent," Fred told them. "Since that's the only tent the Monstrous Mutt hasn't visited yet, we figure he'll show up there soon. We've cleared everyone else out of the ring so they'll be safe," Fred said. "I'll pretend to be the judge while you two go through your paces. When you see the Monstrous Mutt coming, run as fast as you can. Daphne and Velma will be standing by to cut the lines that hold up the tent."

"It's a foolproof plan," said Velma.

"Like, I sure hope so," answered Shaggy.

He and Scooby followed Fred into the tent. They entered the ring together, and Fred began to put them through their paces. "Handler, tell your dog to sit," he said.

"Like, sit, Scooby," Shaggy said.

Scooby just looked at him. Then he pranced off in the opposite direction.

Fred grinned. "Tell your dog to come," he said.

"Scooby, come!" Shaggy called.

Scooby ignored him.

Shaggy ran after him and brought him back.

"Tell your dog to walk next to you in heel position," Fred said.

"Like, heel!" Shaggy said. He started to walk. Scooby came with him, but instead of walking next to Shaggy, he bounded along in front of him.

Velma and I stood near the main ropes. Each of us held large hedge clippers we'd gotten from the maintenance closet. "Scooby's not going to win this trial!" I said, laughing.

Just then, we heard a roar and a clanking sound, coming closer every second. "The Monstrous Mutt!" Velma cried. "Run, Fred! Run, Scooby and Shaggy!"

The Monstrous Mutt drew closer, clanking along until he was underneath the tent.

Meanwhile, Fred, Shaggy, and Scooby took off in the opposite direction. When we were sure they were safely out of the tent, Velma and I each cut a rope.

The huge tent collapsed, catching the Monstrous Mutt in mid-stride. He roared louder and struggled to find his way out of the billowing pile of striped fabric that was trapping him, but it didn't do him any good.

The Monstrous Mutt had been caught.

"**W**ow," you say, taking the last sip of your smoothie. "That was some mystery."

"We're dog-tired, but we solved it!" says Fred with a grin. "I bet you can, too."

"We can help," Velma says. "First, think about each of your suspects. Which of them had the best reason to scare people away from the Major's dog show?"

"Next," Daphne adds, "think about the clues you found. Which of the suspects might have left them?"

"If you can eliminate any suspects, that might help," Fred says.

56

"And it also might help if you, like, buy one of the detectives another smoothie!" Shaggy adds hopefully. "Like, I'm thinking banana-peanut-butter-raspberry supreme!"

"Shaggy!" Daphne says, exasperated. She turns back to you. "Look over my notes one more time. Check the notes in your own Clue Keeper, too. Then, when you're ready, we'll tell you who the Monstrous Mutt really was."

Do you think you know who's behind this mechanical menace? When you think you've solved the mystery, turn the page and find out if you're right.

"It was Harvey Harmon!" Velma says. "The hot-dog man. He was the only suspect who was on hand each time there was a dirty trick or a nasty surprise. And then, when the Monstrous Mutt appeared, Harvey was nowhere in sight! He admitted everything once he discovered we had caught the Monstrous Mutt."

"For a while we thought it was Winifred Slate," Daphne says. "But she was too busy showing off Griselda. And it was only a soda pop bottle she threw away when we heard that *clunk*."

"We also thought could have been Josie

McBee," Fred says, "because she had the theatrical talent to make the Monstrous Mutt look real. But she wasn't around when the cats were let loose."

"There were three clues that led us to Harvey Harmon," Velma tells you. "First, Harvey was around when the chow chow got sprayed with white paint."

"Next, there were those giant empty cans out in back of his trailer," Fred adds. "He used those cans to create the Monstrous Mutt! That's why the Mutt's feet said 'Dog' on them. Because they once held hot-dog relish!"

"The final clue was the cat hair in his trailer," Daphne says. "That was a real giveaway."

"The Major was so happy that we solved the case!" Velma says. "He treated us all to every snack we wanted at the food court."

Scooby and Shaggy pat their round stomachs. "Like, that's right," Shaggy says. "I finally got that blue raspberry sno-cone. And a red cherry one. And a purple blueberry one. And a green lime one."

"Rutti-frutti!" says Scooby.

"That's right!" Shaggy says, laughing. "Tutti-frutti, too! That was the best one of all, with all the flavors, like, mixed together."

Velma rolls her eyes. "You two will eat anything. But I guess you deserved a treat for helping to solve that mystery." She turns to you. "I bet you solved it, too," she says. "But even if you didn't, there's always another mystery to solve!"

"We'll be sure to let you know next time we come across one," Daphne says.

"And in the meantime," Shaggy says, "like, if you come across a dog named Griselda, be sure to tell her that Scooby says . . ."

"Rooby-rooby-roo!" Scooby finishes.

61